the
Swan™
princess

The Swan princess™

A novelization by A.L. Singer
Based on a screenplay by Brian Nissen
From a story by Richard Rich and Brian Nissen

SCHOLASTIC INC.
New York Toronto London Auckland Sydney

ISBN 0-590-22204-X

12 11 10 9 8 7 6 5 4 3 2 1   4 5 6 7 8 9/9

Printed in the U.S.A.   40

First Scholastic printing, November 1994

the Swan™ princess

1

"**O**dette."

King William smiled at the sleeping baby in his arms. Again he whispered, "Odette."

That would be his daughter's name. It meant *wealthy*, for truly that was how he felt. Wealthy in his heart.

For long years King William had ruled the land with wisdom and kindness. He had riches beyond imagination. He had the love of his subjects. Yet for all that, William had been sad and lonely. For although, as King, he loved his people, he had never loved as a father. More than anything, he had longed for a child. And he had given up hope — until this, his sixtieth year.

Until Odette.

He cradled the tiny girl in his arms. Then he walked her toward the royal balcony. Two servants, smiling widely, flung open the glass doors.

Outside, the entire kingdom awaited his news. King William strode to the balcony. With tears in his eyes, he held his daughter for all to see. "Long live Princess Odette!" he cried.

So loud was the cheer from the King's subjects, it could be heard in the next kingdom.

"LONG LIVE THE PRINCESS!"

For weeks afterward, kings and queens arrived to greet the child. All marveled at the baby's beauty. Each day the castle was crowded with courtiers.

On one of those days, the widowed Queen Uberta visited with her young son, Prince Derek.

Derek toddled to Odette's bassinet. He looked inside. A squirming baby, he thought. Big deal.

He dropped a golden locket into the bassinet, just as his mother had asked him. See baby, give locket. That was all he had to do. Now it was done. Time to go home.

When he turned, he saw a room full of people grinning at him. Except for his mother and King William. They were grinning at each other.

In their minds, they were planning his marriage to Odette.

Hidden among the visitors that day was an old, bearded man. To him, the baby Princess meant nothing. His face had no smile. His dark eyes darted around the room. It would all be his some day — the room, the castle, the kingdom.

His name was Rothbart, and he was an Enchanter with an evil plan. By mastering the For-

2

bidden Arts, he would gain the power to take William's kingdom. Day and night he practiced his sorcery in a secret lair, with only the help of a loyal Hag.

News of Rothbart's plan reached King William. On the eve of the attack, the King sent his army to destroy the evil hiding place.

Rothbart and the Hag were brought before William. "Death to the Enchanter!" cried the people of the kingdom.

But William, as always, showed mercy. "I will not take a life," he announced, "however, I hereby banish Rothbart from my kingdom forever."

But Rothbart was far from grateful. "I'm not finished with you yet, Willie," he growled as he was dragged away. "Someday I'll get my power back. And when I do, everything you own, everything you love, will be *mine!*"

2

F*ffffff.* Queen Uberta's Chamberlain tried to blow the royal trumpet, but no sound came out.

Uh-oh. From high atop the castle tower lookout, he squinted into the distance. Yes, that *was* King William's caravan approaching. No doubt about it. And the Queen had *insisted* on a trumpet fanfare for this occasion. Today was to be the first meeting between the young Prince Derek and Princess Odette!

So what was wrong with the trumpet? He tried and tried again: *Fffffff . . . ffffff . . . BLATTTTT!*

A bird and her nest popped out. The trumpet blared and screeched.

Directly below the tower, King William and Princess Odette entered the castle. Queen Uberta received them with open arms. Beside her, Prince Derek scowled.

Derek remembered Odette. He had put the locket in her cradle. Now he was five years old, and she was just *three* — still a baby! He did want to have anything to do with her.

"Dear Uberta," the King said. "As lovely as ever."

Splat.

The bird's nest fell into the Queen's silver-gray hairdo.

But King William hadn't noticed a thing. "And who might this strapping young man be?" he said, patting Derek on the head. "Young Prince Derek, no doubt."

Swoop. The bird snatched her nest off Queen Uberta's head. The Queen growled at the Chamberlain, then turned to King William and smiled. "Welcome to our fair kingdom, dear William," she said. "And to you, young Princess."

The King nudged his daughter forward. Her golden locks bobbed up and down as she walked toward Derek.

Disgusting. That was the first and only word that came to Derek's mind.

"Go on, Derek!" Uberta whispered.

"*Mother!*" Derek whined.

Queen Uberta glowered at him. "*Derek!*"

Derek recognized her *Do this or else* voice. He stepped forward. Then, as quickly and quietly as he could manage, he said, "Hello-Princess-Odette-I-am-very-pleased-to-meet-you."

Odette smiled shyly. "Pleased to meet *you*, Prince Derek."

5

so happy, he could barely feel his feet touch the ground.

Queen Uberta almost fainted with joy.

Through the rest of the summer, Derek and Odette hardly ever left each other's side. Long walks on the castle grounds led to stolen kisses behind the royal gardens.

Derek dreamed of Odette. He awoke each morning eager to see her. When he was with her, he felt overjoyed, but tongue-tied, unable to tell her how he felt.

How could I have ever hated her? he wondered. Hate was the furthest thing from his mind now.

Now, he could not imagine ever living without her.

At summer's end, on the day Odette was to leave, the couple danced all night at a royal ball. Lord Rogers conducted the Royal Orchestra. William and Uberta watched and waited.

No one at the ball could mistake the love that burned in the eyes of Odette and Derek. As they whirled across the dance floor, swept up in their emotions, all guests stopped to admire them.

Odette smiled at her handsome Prince, but inside she felt a tug of sadness. She couldn't bear to leave him. In his shy, quiet way, Derek had given her so much love over the summer — but he had never declared it. Maybe he would tonight. Maybe he'd finally *tell* her how he felt.

For the last song of the night, Lord Rogers brought the orchestra to a rousing finish. Queen Uberta prepared to bid the guests good-bye.

Derek and Odette stopped dancing. They shared a long glance. Then Derek turned to the guests with an enormous, joyous grin.

At the top of his voice, he blurted out: "Arrange the wedding!"

All commotion stopped. Queen Uberta and King William were speechless.

But in that moment of silence, Odette called out, "Wait!"

Cries of happiness caught in the guests' throats. The ballroom remained silent.

"What is it?" Derek pleaded. "You're all I ever wanted. You're beautiful!"

"Thank you," Odette replied. "But . . . what else?"

Surely Derek wanted more than her beauty. In her soul, Odette knew Derek loved her as much as she loved him. All she needed was for him to *say* it. He could whisper it to her, or declare it before the kingdom.

But he stared at her blankly. *"What else?"* he repeated.

"Is beauty all that matters to you?" Odette asked.

King William and Queen Uberta stood, dumbfounded.

Derek swallowed hard. "I . . . uh . . . what else is there?"

Odette's heart sank. She had been wrong, she thought. Derek did not love her at all.

She turned to leave the ballroom, taking the hopes of two kingdoms with her.

The following day, as a crestfallen King William led his daughter away, Derek and Odette barely said goodbye.

Derek watched the King's caravan depart, his eyes red with shock and disappointment.

His mother could offer no comfort. Her smile of farewell gave way to a look of disgust. "All these years of planning, wasted!" she murmured.

She turned away and left her son alone with his grief.

3

"What else is there?" Lord Rogers said the words mockingly as he paced the Royal Sitting Room. "*She* says, 'Is beauty all that matters?' and *you* say, 'What else is there?' "

Derek leaned forward on a chess table, propping his head up with his hands. "It was dumb, I know."

Candles flickered against the growing darkness outside. The rain, pelting against the windows, was not helping Derek's mood.

Across the table, Bromley moved his chess knight closer to Derek's king.

"You should write a book," Rogers continued, " 'How to Offend Women in Five Syllables or Less.' "

"Your turn," Bromley announced.

"I didn't know what else to say," Derek claimed as he moved a bishop.

Grinning, Bromley snatched up one of Derek's pieces. "You lost your queen, Derek!"

Derek sighed. "Ugh. That's twice in one day."

"Think," Rogers urged. "You must see something other than Odette's beauty."

"Of course I do, Rogers!" Derek said. "She's . . . you know. And then . . . it's like . . . I mean, right?"

Lord Rogers rolled his eyes.

"Aw, I don't know how to say it!" Derek finally blurted out. He drummed his fingers on the chessboard. "I know. I'll *prove* it to her. I'll prove my love!"

With that, he lifted his rook and moved it across the board. "Checkmate!" he said with a triumphant smile.

Bromley's jaw hung open. Once again, his best friend had won. Everything Derek wanted, Derek seemed to get.

Well, almost everything.

Miles away, in a dark, secluded forest, a white-bearded man waited behind an oak tree. His eyes were trained on King William's caravan, plodding slowly along the mud-soaked trail.

"Today's the day, Willie," Rothbart whispered, staring at King William's coach. "Everything you own, everything you love, will be mine!"

The rain did not bother Rothbart. He had worked these sixteen years to gain back his magical powers, and nothing could stop him now.

He stepped away from the tree, into the path of the approaching caravan.

Inside the royal carriage, King William shook his head sadly. "I just don't understand," he said to his daughter. "What else did you want him to say?"

"I need to know that he loves me," Odette replied.

Neeeeiigh!

As the horses whinnied and bucked, the carriage lurched to a stop.

"What on earth?" King William turned the door handle and stepped out. Beyond the horses, a caped man was blocking the path. Although the man was in silhouette, King William could recognize the aggressive stance. The slightly hunched posture. Could it be Rothbart? After all these years?

"Stay inside, Odette," he said, closing the carriage door.

The King took a step forward. His guards moved to encircle him, spears drawn.

Rothbart opened his arms. A fireball of light exploded around him. His cape became a pair of leathery black wings, his fingers sharp talons. His wrinkled face stretched forward into the shape of a massive, razor-sharp beak.

Shielding their eyes, the King and his guards

stepped backward. Before them stood a tremendous, hideous animal — the face of a hawk, the wings of a bat, the body of a bear, and the clawed feet of a tiger.

With a deafening roar, the beast attacked.

4

*C*reeeeeak!

Derek, Bromley, and Lord Rogers turned at the noise. Who could be pushing open the castle door at this hour?

With a dull, wet thump, a man slumped onto the floor. His uniform was ripped and muddy, his face covered with bruises.

"It's King William's Captain!" Derek cried.

He ran to the man and propped up his head. Rogers and Bromley rushed to his side.

The Captain struggled to speak. "We . . . we were attacked," he said, his voice a parched whisper. "A Great Animal . . ."

Derek looked out the open door in horror. "Odette!"

He set the Captain down gently and bolted out the door.

"No, Derek!" Lord Rogers shouted after him. "Wait!"

Derek ignored him. He raced to the Royal Stable, jumped onto his horse, and took off.

The horse sent up clods of mud as it galloped through the forest. Derek blinked away raindrops and trained his eyes on the path.

Deep in the woods he spotted the twisted wreckage of a caravan. He brought the horse to a halt and jumped off.

Carriage wheels were strewn about, surrounded by a jumble of splintered carriages.

"Odette?" he cried, pulling open a carriage door.

Empty.

"Uuuuuhhh," a voice behind him moaned.

Derek spun around. Lying against an overturned wagon was King William, bloodied and beaten.

The King's eyes flickered open as Derek rushed to his side. "Who did this?" Derek said, propping King William's head on his lap.

"It came . . . so quickly," the King struggled to say. "A Great Animal . . ."

"Where is Odette?" Derek pleaded.

His voice fading, King William said, "Listen to me, Derek. It's not what it seems . . . it's not what it seems . . ."

"What's not? *Where is Odette?*"

"Odette . . ." The King winced with pain. He wet his lips and murmured, "Odette . . . is . . . *gone.*"

King William's eyes shut. His head rolled to one side and his body became limp and lifeless.

Derek placed the old man's body on the ground. Rearing his head back, he let out a cry of anguish. The cry of a boy who has lost everything.

"ODETTE!"

5

In a dark, lost corner of the forest, the moon rose over a decrepit castle. Although the rain had stopped, water poured from the crumbling turrets and gables.

Attached to this castle was a tall tower dungeon, surrounded by a moat. Beyond that was a stone floor, ending in a set of stone stairs that led downward to a lake.

On that lake, a lonely swan glided.

Rothbart and the Hag happily tossed bread crumbs to the majestic white bird. "Aw, don't let my little spell make you sad, Odette," he said. "It doesn't last the whole day. As soon as the moon comes up — "

He didn't need to finish. Creeping across the lake, the moonlight touched the swan's wing. Water began to swirl up from below. The swan rose upward in a shimmering geyser of light and transformed into Princess Odette.

"And that's how it works every night," Rothbart said, as Odette landed gently on the shore. "You have to be on the lake, of course, and when the moonlight touches your wings — you're human!"

Odette turned away from him. All she could think about was her father. She would never forgive Rothbart for what he'd done.

"Look, Odette," Rothbart went on, "this sort of thing doesn't give me any pleasure — well, maybe a *teensy* bit — but what I really want is your father's kingdom."

"With all your power, why don't you just take it?" Odette retorted.

"Nah, I tried that already. Once you steal something, you spend your whole life fighting to keep it." Rothbart moved closer, grinning. "*But* . . . if I marry the only heir to the throne, we can rule together — legally! King and Queen!"

Odette couldn't believe her ears. "Never!"

She shoved him aside and stomped away toward the forest.

Rothbart laughed. "Where are you going? As soon as the moonlight leaves the lake, you'll turn back into a swan — no matter where you are!"

Odette stopped. On foot she'd never make it out of the forest in time.

She turned back to Rothbart, frozen in her tracks. She was his prisoner now.

Hidden behind a nearby tree, a frog and a turtle watched sadly.

"Looks like she's going to be here for a while, Speed," said the frog.

"Poor girl," groaned the turtle.

Prince Derek searched through the wreckage, but found no sign of Odette. Could she be alive? Was she being held a prisoner? Who — or what — was the Great Animal?

He vowed he would hunt the creature down.

Derek barely slept that night. At sunrise he ordered Lord Rogers to arrange a Royal Target Practice.

In it, Derek and Bromley used soft, harmless arrows, each with a powder-puff tip. Derek's arrows were dipped in orange powder, Bromley's in blue — to leave a mark for each hit. The court musicians, dressed as animals, ran through the woods and tried to avoid being hit.

Derek did not miss one shot.

The musicians, covered with orange spots, were not happy about this. Neither was Lord Rogers.

"Oh, Derek," he said with an exasperated sigh. "You've looked everywhere. You know Odette's not coming back. The whole kingdom knows that."

"The whole kingdom is wrong," Derek shot back. He spun on his heels and walked off the field.

"You're a great marksman, Derek," Bromley said, putting his arm around his friend's shoulder.

"But it takes more than good aim. It takes courage. That's my forte."

Behind them, Lord Rogers piped up, "Well, then, how about a quick round of Catch and Fire?"

Bromley's face turned green. "C-C-C-Catch and Fire? Me?"

"You're the only one with enough c-c-c-courage," Rogers said with a smile.

Bromley had never tried Catch and Fire. He had hoped he never would. But now he was stuck.

Rogers and Derek disappeared into the castle armory and returned with two bows, one arrow, a suit of armor, and an apple.

Shaking, Bromley donned the armor and picked up the bow and arrow. Rogers placed the apple atop Bromley's helmet.

Across the field, Derek stood with his back turned.

Bromley lifted the bow and aimed the arrow at Derek's back. "What if I — ?" he whimpered.

"Remember, now, aim for the heart," Rogers replied calmly. "Right between the shoulders."

"Oh, please . . . oh, please . . . oh, please . . ." Bromley muttered. He stretched the arrow back and let fly. *"Now!"* he screeched as the arrow flew toward Derek — right on target.

At the last second Derek whirled around. In one motion he grabbed the arrow in midflight, loaded it onto his own bow, and shot it back toward Bromley.

Zzzzzing!

Bromley closed his eyes. He gritted his teeth.

Crunch!

Above his head, the arrow split the apple neatly in two.

Bromley's knees buckled and he fell to the ground.

Lord Rogers caught a chunk of apple and took a bite. "Well done, Derek!" he cried.

Dazed, Bromley struggled to rise up.

"Extraordinary courage, man!" Rogers said to him. "Just think, an inch lower and that arrow would have — "

Bromley thought about it. Then he fell to the ground in a dead faint.

Derek gazed into the forest beyond the field. "Hold on, Odette," he said under his breath. "I'm going to find you."

6

"**Q**uiet!" said Jean-Bob, the frog. "I cannot con-
centrate."

Speed, the turtle, tried not to laugh.

Jean-Bob took hold of the long, strung-together
cattails and prepared to pole-vault. Sure, he could
hop great distances by himself — but not all the
way across the moat to the tall tower, Rothbart's
water dungeon.

At the tower's base, in a clump of mud above
the water line, grew the most perfect flowers
Jean-Bob had ever seen. For the Princess, he
would risk his life to snatch those flowers. He
would vault above the heads of the hungry alligators.

"You've come up with some dumb ideas, Jean-
Bob," Speed said, "but this one is a doozy."

Jean-Bob dusted himself off. "Go ahead and
laugh," he said, picking some more cattails from
the ground. "I'll get that Princess to kiss me, and
when she does — "

"Poof, you'll change into a French Prince," Speed finished. "I know, I know, you've told me."

"When she learns zat I have risked my life for those flowers, ze kissing will not stop!" Jean-Bob smiled as he attached three more strong cattails together. The pole had to be perfect.

Speed had heard Jean-Bob's Frog-Prince story a hundred times. He'd given up telling Jean-Bob how ridiculous it sounded. "Mind if I point out a problem?" Speed asked.

"I don't take advice from *peasants*," Jean-Bob sniffed.

"Suit yourself," Speed replied.

Jean-Bob balanced his cattail pole. He hunched over, closed his eyes, and chanted softly: "Flowers, kiss, concentration . . . flowers, kiss, concentration . . ."

Then, opening his eyes, he ran toward the moat. He planted the pole and leaped.

Whoooosh! Up over the moat he sailed.

"Just curious how you're going to get back," Speed said.

Jean-Bob's eyes went wide. Below him, the teeth of a dozen alligators gleamed. The pole was taking him down, down, down . . .

SNNNNAP! went an alligator jaw. It was so close, Jean-Bob could smell the bad breath.

"Yeaaaaagh!" he shrieked.

The pole now sprang him back to dry land. "Waaaaagh! Speed! Stop me!" Jean-Bob pleaded.

24

Speed inched forward and tried to grab Jean-Bob in vain.

Sproiing! Back he went to the water.

The alligators jumped.

Sproiing! Back to land.

"Help! Help, you sluggard!" Jean-Bob cried.

Back and forth he swung, dropping closer and closer to the waiting jaws. He closed his eyes. He was alligator meat now. He would never live to see Odette, never become a Prince, never inherit a kingdom. Never . . .

He wasn't moving.

He was still.

Was this what death felt like . . . no pain, just dullness? Emptiness?

He opened his eyes. A gasp caught in his throat.

Odette — the Princess herself — was holding the tip of the cattail in her hand. She had stopped the swinging.

And she was smiling *at him*!

"Odette!" Jean-Bob exclaimed. He jumped off the cattail and bowed. "Oh, thank you, thank you!"

"*Sssss! Sssss!*" hissed the angry alligators behind him.

Jean-Bob turned to face them. Grabbing the cattail, he brought it down on the alligators like a whip. "*Ha!*"

Thwap! The cattail sprang back and smacked him on the head.

25

"Are you all right?" Odette asked.

"Yes, Odette," Jean-Bob groaned. "I am all right."

"What in the world were you trying to do?"

Speed chuckled. "He thought that if — "

"Shush!" Jean-Bob snapped. Then, chin raised high, he said to Odette, "I wanted to get zose flowers for you."

Odette raised a suspicious eyebrow. "You're being sneaky again, Jean-Bob."

"What sneaky? You deserve a nice bouquet."

"And you deserve a kiss?"

Jean-Bob offered his cheek. "Well, all right. If you insist."

"Give it up, Jean-Bob," Speed remarked.

Odette smiled at Jean-Bob. "You know I'm under a spell," Odette said.

"But my kiss will break ze spell!" Jean-Bob insisted.

Odette shook her head. "I can only kiss the man I love, and then he — "

"Must make a vow of everlasting love," Jean-Bob cut in.

"*And* prove it to the world!" Odette added.

"What do you think *I* was doing with ze flowers and ze alligators, going back and forth? Everlasting love!" Jean-Bob sniffed indignantly. "I was almost everlasting *lunch!*"

"Speed, make him understand," Odette begged.

"I'm only a turtle," Speed replied.

A sudden crash stopped their conversation. Lying on the ground a few yards away, an arrow jutting from its wing, was a small black-and-white bird.

Odette, Jean-Bob, and Speed gathered around it.

"You think he's dead?" Speed asked.

"No," Odette answered. "It's just his wing, I think."

"Strange-looking bird," Jean-Bob remarked.

"Poor fellow," Odette said. "He must be in a lot of pain."

Tenderly she examined the bird's injured wing. "You better hold him," she suggested to Speed.

As Speed sat on the bird's chest, Jean-Bob held down its beak.

"Ready," Speed said.

With a quick snap, Odette broke the arrow. Then, gingerly, she pulled it out. Tearing a strip of cloth from her dress, she wrapped the wing.

Slowly the bird's eyes opened.

"Hello," Jean-Bob sang, "zis is your wake-up call."

With a jerk, the bird sat up.

"Waaagh!" Jean-Bob flew through the air and banged against a tree.

Speed went spinning on his shell.

The bird stood, ready to fight. "Ha! It takes more than a pair of pond punks to keep Puffin down! Ha!"

"I'm your friend!" Odette said.

"Friend, my feathers!" Puffin replied. "I have a background in logic, Madam! If you're my *friend*, how come you have an arrow in your hand?" He snatched the arrow from Odette. "The exact kind of arrow I have — "

Puffin stopped. He stared at his wing. "What — ?"

"I took it out while you were lying here," Odette said.

"You mean, you had a chance to *kkkkkkk* — " With his wing tip, Puffin made a slitting gesture across his throat. " — and instead you *ffffft?*" He pantomimed pulling an arrow out.

"Uh-huh." Odette tried not to giggle. She'd never met anyone who spoke in sound effects.

Puffin smiled. "Madam, I may be schooled in the strategies of war, but I'm also schooled in manners. I apologize. My name is Puffin. Lieutenant Puffin."

"It's a pleasure. I'm Odette. Princess Odette." Odette held out her hand, and Puffin kissed it.

"And these are my best friends in the whole world," Odette continued. "Mister Lorenzo Trudgealong — "

"Friends call me Speed," Speed said.

" — and Jean-Bob."

Jean-Bob bowed deeply. "I have no friends, only servants, and *they* call me 'Your Highness.' " He held out *his* hand to be kissed.

28

"He thinks he's a prince," Speed explained.

"Well!" Puffin said, ignoring Jean-Bob. "I owe you, Princess, and I intend on staying until my debt is paid."

"I don't think there's much you can do," Odette replied. "He has me under a spell."

"You mean, a magical . . ." Puffin waved his wings. *"Fsht-fsht?"*

In an instant, the dark forest became bright as day. The gnarled trees bloomed with cherry blossoms. Rothbart appeared, dressed in full armor, holding his helmet in his hand.

"Your knight in shining armor has come to set you free!" he said with a mocking laugh.

Puffin stepped up to fight Rothbart, but Speed and Jean-Bob pulled him back.

"Let me at him!" Puffin shouted. "I'll *psssh!* And I'll *kkkkg!* And I'll — "

Speed squeezed Puffin's beak shut.

Rothbart bent down on one knee. "All it takes is one word, Odette. Will you marry me?"

"Every night you ask the same question," Odette replied. "And every night I give you the same answer. I'll *die* first!"

Rothbart scowled. Instantly the sky darkened and the forest plunged into a deep gloom.

"Ooh, you're really starting to bug me," Rothbart said.

"I should think you'd be used to it now," Odette retorted.

"That's it — just keep pushing it!" Rothbart snapped. "Someday I'm going to boil over!"

"Go ahead, then. But I'll never give you my father's kingdom!"

Rothbart was fuming. He bit his finger to control his emotions. Then, practically spitting his words out, he said, "I was hoping you'd say you'd be mine, but it looks as if you need another day to think about it."

As Rothbart turned back toward his castle, Odette sank to the ground.

She would never marry that . . . that *murderer*! She would remain a swan forever if she had to.

Burying her head in her hands, she burst into tears.

7

"**B**eautiful," Queen Uberta whispered. "Simply beautiful."

Lord Rogers handed Queen Uberta the crown, and she lifted it high. Years ago, after the King had died, Uberta had put away his crown for safekeeping. She had almost forgotten how it looked. Soon her son would be wearing it.

Sunlight poured into the Room of the Crown Jewels. It bounced against the sapphires, rubies, and emeralds in the crown, sending off flares of light.

"Soon Derek will be married and the kingdom will have a king again," Uberta said.

"I doubt it," Rogers replied. "Derek still refuses to be king unless he finds Odette."

"Poppycock! All that will change at tomorrow night's ball."

Wham! The door slammed open and the Chamberlain barged in. He was smiling so hard, his chubby cheeks seemed ready to crack. "They're all coming!" he said. "Every princess is coming!"

He turned toward the door and clapped his hands. Two servants stepped inside, each carrying a bulging mailbag.

Turning the bags over, they dumped piles of envelopes on the Chamberlain's head.

Uberta ran to the Chamberlain and took a handful of letters.

Replies — they were all replies! All saying yes!

"Oh ho! This is wonderful!" Uberta exclaimed. "You see, Rogers, *one* of these young ladies is bound to change Derek's mind."

"Oh, absolutely . . ." Rogers replied. To himself, he added, *"Not."*

"Do not lose one of these replies!" Uberta commanded the Chamberlain, walking away with a batch of them.

"But — " the Chamberlain protested.

"Now, where is Derek? Oh, I know where he is — in the library, working on the mystery of the Fat Animal."

"Uh, the *Great* Animal, Your Highness," Rogers corrected her.

"Oh, Big, Great, Fat, whatever," the Queen said. "It's large and it has fur."

In the second-floor library, Prince Derek climbed a ladder to the top bookshelf. He pulled out a thick, musty book and blew dust off the cover.

He read the title: *Beasts and Spirits of the Night*.

This could be it, he thought. He began flipping through the pages. " 'It's not what it seems . . . it's not what it seems . . .' What did King William mean?"

Finally his fingers stopped at a chapter titled, "Animal Transformations."

As he scanned through the pages, his face lit up. "It's not what it seems — of course!" Quickly he ripped out a handful of pages and clutched them tightly. "*Now* I'll find you, Odette!"

He leaped off the ladder. His feet hit the floor near the library entrance — and he came face to face with his mother.

"Oh!" Queen Uberta cried. She jumped back, dropping some of the letters she'd been carrying.

Derek spun her around and ran out of the library.

"Where are you going, Derek?" Uberta demanded.

"To find the Great Animal!" Derek replied, waving the ripped-out pages high. "I figured it out!"

"Wonderful. Just make sure you're here for tomorrow night."

Huh? Derek stopped and turned around. "Tomorrow night?"

"The *ball*!" Uberta reminded him.

"Mother, I — I can't."

Uberta's face fell. Her eyes began to water. As she held back tears, her lips quivered.

"Please, Mother, don't do the lip thing!"

Uberta put her hands to her lips, but it was hopeless. They had a life of their own. She started to sob.

Derek sighed. "All right . . . if I leave now, maybe I can get back in time."

His mother broke into a huge smile, throwing the letters into the air with joy.

"But please, Mother, don't turn this into one of your big beauty pageants."

"Oh, no, no, no," Uberta insisted. "It's just a few friends . . ."

Nodding, Derek dashed out of the library.

When he was out of sight, Uberta finished her sentence. ". . . and their daughters."

The Chamberlain came huffing and puffing into the room, scooping up letters.

"I want this to be big!" the Queen exclaimed. "Every princess must have her own introduction — "

"But you said — "

"Forget what I said! Now, send for the cooks and tell the band to start rehearsing. And I want four footmen for every carriage . . ."

"Yes, Your Highness," the Chamberlain grumbled.

The color drained from his face. This was going to be the hardest day of his life.

8

Puffin watched the last trace of the moon disappear behind the lake. He had just seen the Princess transform, but he could hardly believe his eyes.

"Let me get this straight," he said to the sleek white swan Odette had become. "Every night, when the moonlight leaves the lake, you . . . *quack!*"

Odette barely left a ripple in the still water as she swam. "Right," she replied. "The following night, if I want to change back to a human, I have to be on the lake."

"All *she* needs is a little moonlight," Jean-Bob said with a sigh. "*Me*, I have to be smooched."

Puffin thought hard. There had to be a way . . .

"I got it!" he blurted out. "We'll find Derek and lure him back to the lake!"

The others stared at him blankly.

"We get here just as the moon is coming up,"

Puffin went on. "The Prince comes through the forest, you change into a Princess . . . happy ever after!"

"How would I find him?" Odette asked.

Now it was Puffin's turn to look confused. "You mean, you don't know where he is?"

"I don't even know where *I* am," Odette answered.

Speed glanced at Rothbart's castle. "I bet *he* does."

"Oh, that's a *great* idea," Jean-Bob said with a laugh. "Just say, 'Monsieur Rothbart, I'd like to leave now. Do you have a map or something?' "

"A map!" Puffin and Odette exclaimed together. "That's it!"

Jean-Bob gasped. They couldn't mean . . .

"Let's do it," Odette said.

She turned in the direction of the castle and began to fly. Puffin ran along, testing his injured wing. Speed crawled after them.

What did I get us into? Jean-Bob said to himself. His heart sinking, he hopped toward the castle.

Odette soared over the deterioration. Below her, sections of castle roof had rotted away. Turrets sloped dangerously, and the windows that remained were covered with thick grime.

Through a fourth-floor window, Odette spotted the outline of a map hanging on the wall. She flew down to tell the others.

"All right," Puffin said. "Odette will keep a look-out while we get the map."

"I don't like ze way you use ze word *we*," Jean-Bob groused.

"You're not going to help us?" Puffin asked.

"*Oui!*" Jean-Bob replied.

Together, the three of them approached the main door of the castle. It was hanging ajar, so they pushed.

Eeeeeeeee. It squeaked open, revealing a dusty, dimly lit room. Against the opposite wall, a curved staircase led upward into darkness.

"Quickly," Puffin urged.

"Easy for you to say," drawled Speed.

As Puffin and Jean-Bob scampered inside, the heavy wooden door slammed on Speed.

"Ouch," he moaned.

From the top of the grand staircase, candlelight flickered.

Frantically Jean-Bob and Puffin pulled Speed inside. Then they darted into a corner to hide, leaving Speed to crawl after them.

The Hag came into view at the top of the stairs. Slowly she descended, swinging a candelabra from side to side.

As she reached the bottom step, Speed walked into her path.

"Oh, zis is great," Jean-Bob whispered to Puffin. "Whenever I have to do something quick, I always like to bring a turtle."

Whap-whap-whap-whap-whap!

Jean-Bob and Puffin saw Odette flapping her wings against a window. As the Hag turned away from Speed to look, Odette flew away.

Whap-whap-whap-whap-whap! This time Odette pounded on another window, just out of the Hag's sight.

Jean-Bob and Puffin sneaked up the stairs — second floor, third floor . . .

Behind them, Speed groaned, "I think I pulled a muscle."

At the fourth floor, near a rusted suit of armor, Jean-Bob stopped and looked back. "I'm going to die, I know it!" he said, smacking his head in frustration. "I'm on a dangerous mission with a lame turtle. Speed, you're going to get us all killed."

As he swung his arm down, he smacked the suit of armor.

CLANK!

It toppled over. Despite his lame wing, Puffin managed to fly away. Jean-Bob got stuck in a boot and hopped away inside it.

Thump-thump-thump-thump! The Hag ran up the stairs. Jean-Bob and Puffin disappeared into the map room, where Speed was patiently waiting.

"Beat you," he droned.

Whap-whap!

Odette was at the window. Puffin leaped, flapping his wings. He could do it! His injury was feeling much better than he expected. He flew to Odette and let her in.

"Good, you made it!" Odette said, trying to squeeze through the small opening.

"Wait here and we'll hand you the map," Puffin ordered.

He flew to the map and lifted it off its hook. Jean-Bob positioned himself underneath.

The map slammed to the floor. With a sharp snap, it rolled Jean-Bob up inside.

Speed and Puffin quickly pulled him out. Then, grabbing the map in his beak, Puffin dashed for the window.

Thoonk! A gnarled hand pushed the window shut.

The Hag!

Puffin gasped. "Head for the door!" he cried.

The Hag was faster than she looked. She sped to the door and blocked it.

The three animals huddled. "All right," Puffin said. "Jean-Bob goes deep. Speed, stop the rush. We need this one, guys. Ready . . . *break!*"

Speed took the map and crouched into a line of scrimmage with Jean-Bob.

"Green! Nineteen! Set! Hut!" Puffin barked.

Speed hiked the map. Puffin ran toward the Hag, then lateraled to Speed.

"I'm open!" Jean-Bob shouted.

Speed passed to Jean-Bob. The Hag went back

to intercept. Jean-Bob leaped. He grabbed the map out of her clutches.

"Weee-heee!" Jean-Bob squealed.

The Hag lifted him upward. She pulled the map from his hand and used it to whack him back to Puffin.

Puffin glanced around the room. He picked up a pan lying nearby.

Whomp! He smacked Jean-Bob back toward the Hag. "Get the map!" he yelled.

In midair, Jean-Bob took the map out of the Hag's hand and sailed out the door.

Jean-Bob sprawled on the floor, then sprinted away, leaping over a low stool . . . a high stool . . . ahead of him loomed a dark, wooden bannister. He *knew* he could clear it. He planted his feet and sprang.

He sailed over the bannister — and plunged downward to the third floor.

Oops.

Fooosh! Speed swung by on a rope and caught Jean-Bob in his stubby arm.

"Saved you," he said.

They landed on the floor below. Directly in front of the Hag — who was holding a broom over her head, ready to strike.

"Thanks a lot," Jean-Bob said, running off with the map.

Across the room, Puffin was waiting. Jean-Bob

passed the map to him like a relay runner. Puffin took flight, looking over his shoulder for the Hag, and —

Thump. He crashed against the wall and fell.

Ninety feet away, Speed crouched into a baseball catcher's position. "Ay, batter, batter, batter!" he cried.

The Hag stepped in front of him and lifted her broom into batting position.

Puffin took signs from Speed, went into a windup, and pitched the map. The Hag swung and missed. Speed caught it and held tight.

"He did it!" Puffin yelled. "The crowd's going wild!"

But so was the Hag. She swatted Speed with her broom, trying to get the map away.

Against the wall, Puffin spotted a bucket of water and a mop. He spilled the water, then slid across the slippery floor toward the Hag.

Wham! He gave her a shoulder check.

The Hag barely moved. With a slight shift of her hips, she sent Puffin flying across the room.

"Oof!" Puffin yelled.

The Hag eyed Jean-Bob, who was cowering by the stairs. Using her broom, she slapped Speed as if he were a hockey puck, right toward Jean-Bob.

"Aaaagh!" Jean-Bob shrieked, hopping for his life.

He came down on Speed's back. Now the *two* of them were gliding over the floor. Speed curled up into his shell, still holding the map.

"Whoa! Whoa!" Jean-Bob steered Speed around the room. They barreled toward Puffin. Jean-Bob closed his eyes.

Puffin leaped. He landed on Speed. Now he *and* Jean-Bob were riding the turtle.

Speed shot onto a curved bannister. The three of them slid downward to the second floor. "Lean to the left!" Puffin called out. "Lean to the right!" Then, for good measure, he added, "Stand up, sit down, fight, fight, fight!"

With a thump, the Hag jumped onto the bannister behind them. *"Hag at six o'clock!"* Puffin shouted.

Zzzzing! They zipped off the end of the bannister. Jean-Bob's eyes widened. *"Wall at noon!"* he screamed.

The Hag launched herself into the air. She lunged, arms outstretched.

SMMMAAASHHH! The three animals rocketed through a window, into the open air.

The Hag missed. She thudded against the wall and dropped to the floor.

Puffin, Jean-Bob, and Speed were soaring. "We're home free!" Puffin crowed. He flapped his wings and flew away from the castle.

Jean-Bob and Speed plummeted. Below them,

alligators circled in the moat. They lifted their bodies out of the water, mouths open, teeth gleaming.

"Yikes," Speed said.

"*Aaaaagh!*" Jean-Bob shrieked. What a way for a prince to die!

9

The map!
Jean-Bob grabbed it from Speed and held it over his head. It billowed out like a parachute.

Speed reached for Jean-Bob's legs in vain. He plunged downward. "Save me," he mumbled.

Puffin swooped down. He tried to lift Speed, but only managed to push the turtle toward the shore.

They tumbled to the dirt, bruised but safe.

"Not one of my better landings," Speed remarked.

In the moat, the alligators snapped their jaws in anticipation. Jean-Bob was dropping closer . . . closer . . .

Jean-Bob puffed out his cheeks and blew upward. Maybe he could keep the parachute afloat, maybe he could blow it toward the shore.

Snap! Snap!

Then again, maybe not.

Fffff . . . ffffff . . . Jean-Bob blew as hard as he

could. It was no use. The only place he was going was down. He closed his eyes and gulped.

The bite didn't feel so bad. In fact, he only felt a little jolt. Then he seemed to be floating, on a bed of soft feathers.

Jean-Bob opened his eyes. He screamed.

He *was* floating. On the back of Odette.

She craned her neck and smiled at him. Jean-Bob held on tightly while she landed on the shore.

"Jean-Bob, you made it!" Puffin exclaimed.

Jean-Bob couldn't answer. His teeth were chattering too hard.

On a flat patch of dirt, Speed had rolled out the map. Odette walked over and gazed at it. "There's Derek's kingdom!" she said, pointing with her beak. "When do we leave?"

Puffin leaned over the map. "We must have a plan . . ."

At a campsite in the forest, Prince Derek threw down a page he had ripped out of his book. A picture of a mouse.

Bromley bit into an apple and examined the picture. "It's a mouse," he said.

"No." Derek shook his head. "It's the Great Animal."

Bromley laughed. "A tad small, wouldn't you say?"

"Yeah. Until it changes into this." Derek laid

out three more pictures. In each one, the mouse was larger, more hideous. In the last, it had taken on the shape of an enormous beast.

"It's an animal that can change its shape," Derek explained. "A harmless creature approaches, then suddenly it's too late!"

"You mean, it could be anything."

"Anything."

Bromley stared at the pictures, dumbfounded. A *mouse*? It seemed too ridiculous to be true.

But he believed it. Derek was no fool.

And with that monster loose in the forest, Bromley would make sure never to leave Derek's side.

The two boys mounted their horses. With their bows and quivers slung on their backs, they rode toward the forest.

As Puffin made final plans, Speed floated lazily on the lake. Jean-Bob lay on Speed's back, and Odette swam beside them.

"I apologize for ze way I've been acting, Odette," Jean-Bob said.

"It's all right, Jean-Bob," Odette insisted.

"No, no. Zis Derek, he's important to you, and all I can do is think of myself. Please, Odette, accept my apology."

Odette smiled. "Okay. I accept."

"Good. Now, let's kiss and make up!"

"*Jean-Bob!*" Odette and Speed both scolded.

Jean-Bob looked hurt. "What? What did I say? What?"

On the shore, Puffin stood and cleared his throat. "Ahem! Atten-*hut!*"

Odette and Speed snapped upright in the water. Jean-Bob went flying.

"It's zero hour, troops!" Puffin shouted. "Odette, prepare for takeoff!"

"Right," Odette replied.

"The rest of you have your assignments back here on land," Puffin insisted. "Is everyone ready?"

"Ready for action, sir," Speed said.

"How about you, Jean-Bob?" Puffin asked.

Jean-Bob whistled, absently looking off in another direction.

Puffin took a deep breath. "How about you, *Your Highness?*"

Jean-Bob smiled. "*Oui*, I am ready!"

"Take off!" Puffin bellowed.

Beating their wings mightily, he and Odette took to the air.

"Good luck," Speed said. "Have a nice flight!"

"Be careful," Jean-Bob called out. "If anything happens to her, I'll have you flogged, whipped, put on ze rack — and zen have your legs fried in butter!"

Bromley was shaking. He and Derek were entering the forest now. Even in the daytime, the

47

place was dark. And not only that, it was full of creatures. Full of possible disguises for the Great Animal.

At this point, it wasn't exactly on Bromley's top ten list of areas to visit.

"He's in here, Brom," Derek said, dismounting. "I can feel it."

"How will you know the Great Animal when you see it?" Bromley asked. "I mean, it could be anything."

Derek's face was determined, unquestioning. "I'll know. Better stay close."

Bromley jumped off his horse and stood shoulder-to-shoulder with Derek. "If you say so."

Quietly Derek walked into the forest. Bromley followed him step for step.

Derek stopped and looked around. Bromley stopped, too. Did Derek hear something? What was that shadow behind the dead pine tree? His eyes like two saucers, Bromley gazed around cautiously.

When he turned back, Derek was gone.

"Derek?" Bromley squeaked. *"Derek, where are you?"*

Half-hidden in the shadows ahead, Derek whirled around. "Shhh."

"S-sorry."

Derek scampered among the trees like a cat. Bromley stumbled behind, panting, looking for anything that might possibly be a disguise for . . .

Bzzzzzz.

A dragonfly floated past Bromley.

It could be anything. The words were etched in Bromley's mind. He picked an arrow from his quiver, loaded his bow, and took aim.

Bzzzzzz.

"Derek . . ." Bromley whispered. "Derek?"

Bzzzzzz. The dragonfly was coming closer to Bromley's nose.

"Derek!"

Ziinnng! Bromley let the arrow go. It missed the dragonfly and shot through the branches nearby.

High above the forest, Odette and Puffin flew steadily toward Derek's castle. Puffin's wing felt as strong as ever now.

But Odette was nervous. "You don't think there could be any hunters, do you?" she asked.

"At ease, Odette," Puffin replied. "I can smell a human a mile away."

Ziinnng!

The arrow passed so close, Odette could feel a breeze. She and Puffin both let out a scream.

"Where did that come from?" Puffin said.

"DE-RRREK!"

Odette recognized the voice — Bromley's! "Derek . . ." she repeated. "He's here!"

"You will not lose control," Puffin commanded. "You will follow the plan as outlined."

But Odette wasn't listening. Desperately her eyes searched the area below for a sign — any sign — of her beloved.

Puffin flew under her, blocking her view. "Acknowledge, Odette! Acknowledge!"

Odette maneuvered around him. She dove downward, into the heart of the forest.

"*Odette!*" Puffin called, racing after her.

Not far away, Bromley walked quietly on the fallen pine needles. He tensed his bow, lining up his prey along the shaft of his arrow.

A mouse cowered against a rock, trapped.

"I've got you now!" Bromley gloated. "Don't give me that innocent look! Go ahead, transform! I'm not afraid of you!"

The mouse shivered with fright. He let out a tiny *squeak*.

Bromley dropped his bow. "Aaaaaaaaagh!" he screamed, high-tailing it into the woods.

Derek didn't hear his friend's scream. He was concentrating. Above the treetops was a golden-white flash of light. It was moving toward him, shimmering as it passed around tangled branches.

He took cover behind a tree, out of sight. Quietly, quickly, he put an arrow to his bowstring.

Now he heard a flapping of great wings. He raised his bow, ready for the shot. From the sound of it, he'd have to be quick.

He peeked out from behind the tree and aimed. In his sight, flying toward him at great speed, was a majestic white bird.

Derek lowered his bow. A swan? Why on earth was a *swan* flying through the woods?

Of course, he said to himself. *It's not what it seems. It's not what it seems!*

This was a trap. It had to be. "Just a little closer," he murmured. "Come on . . . come on . . ."

There. It was close enough now. Sure shot.

He stepped out from the tree, lining the swan in his sight. With all his strength, he pulled the bowstring taut.

This one he would not miss.

"This one," he announced out loud, "is for Odette!"

Derek let go. The arrow sliced the air, dead on target!

10

"*O* *dette!*"
The shout tore Puffin's throat. He hurtled downward.

BOOM! His body made contact with Odette's. The two of them jolted away from each other.

Whizzzz! Derek's arrow winged between them, slicing branches off the trees.

Odette regained her balance, then took to the sky. She beat her wings furiously, staring straight ahead.

"That was close!" Puffin said, struggling to catch up.

"We never planned that!" Odette replied.

Puffin looked down. He saw Derek racing after them, following their shadows.

"The plan is working!" Puffin cried out. "Here he comes!"

When he looked back up, Odette was far in front of him.

"Hey, slow down!" Puffin yelled. "You're going to lose him!"

He flew as hard as he could. With a desperate lunge, he grabbed her feet. "You're going to leave your prince in the dust!" he insisted, climbing wing-over-wing up Odette's back.

But Odette wouldn't listen. Fear propelled her forward. Fear for her life.

Her mind was a jumble of frantic thoughts. Derek hadn't recognized her. Of course not. She hadn't expected him to. So why had she flown so close to him? Why hadn't she followed Puffin's plan — to lure Derek back to the lake?

Now he was after her. But why? *Why did he want to shoot her?* And what had he meant by saying "This one's for Odette"?

Puffin clawed his way over her back, leaning forward to look over her head and into her eyes. *"Slow down!"*

"It's too dangerous!" Odette replied.

"Too dangerous? He can't even see us anymore, let alone — "

Ziinnng! An arrow shot between Puffin's legs.

"Aaaagh! Speed up, girl!" Puffin glanced below and saw the top of Derek's head directly underneath them. "That boy of yours can move!"

"He's too close, Puffin!" Odette cried.

"Don't worry, Odette. I've been taught just what to do in this situation."

Now Derek had found a clearing, with a clear

sight line to Odette. With a look of grim determination, he was setting up a shot.

"Well?" Odette demanded.

"I'm thinking! I'm thinking!"

Derek pulled back his bowstring again.

"*PUFFIN!*"

"Oh, yeah! 'When the archer has you in his sight, fly into the sun and use its light.' Follow me!"

To their left, the setting sun had swollen to a bright orange globe. Together Puffin and Odette flew directly into it.

Puffin glanced quickly behind. Derek was shielding his eyes, his bow lowered to his side.

"Ha ha!" Puffin laughed. "What did I tell you, Odette? Now all we have to do is stay in the sun."

They were able to do that for about two minutes. The sun seemed to flatten against the horizon, then dropped out of sight.

Puffin and Odette both gasped.

"All right, don't panic!" Puffin insisted. "Don't panic!"

Below them Derek emerged from a dense grove of trees. He climbed a rock, planted his feet, and lined up his sights.

"*Odette!*" Puffin shrieked.

With blinding quickness, Derek released another shot.

"Into the trees!" Odette said.

They dropped to the branches below. The arrow whizzed by them again.

Crying out in frustration, Derek jumped off the rock and onto a tree. He climbed into the branches and looked around.

Puffin and Odette flew low. Derek was well above them now.

Silently they glided onto a branch below Derek. They were hidden well by the dense, berry-covered foliage.

"I hope you know what to do now," Odette whispered. "Because if you don't, we're dead ducks."

Puffin nodded solemnly. " 'All birds should remember,' the Possum said, 'when there's no escape, you have to play dead.' "

He plucked a berry, put it between his teeth, and bit down.

Bright red juice spattered his white-feathered belly. "Gives it the right touch," he said with a wink. "Now, wait till I give you the signal."

Puffin fell backward, off the branch. He landed on the forest floor with a dull thump.

"Squaawwk! Ack! Ack!" Puffin cried, staggering around in make-believe pain. With a final scream, he collapsed and lay still.

Derek climbed down. He tiptoed closer, his brow furrowed.

Through squinted eyes, Puffin saw Derek's foot edging nearer, ready to nudge him.

Snap!

Puffin clamped his beak down on Derek's toe.

"YEOOWW!" Derek grabbed his foot and hopped in pain.

Puffin took to the sky. *"CAAAAAAW!"* he trumpeted.

The signal. Odette unfurled her wings and flew as fast as she could.

The two of them soared over the darkening countryside. "That'll put some distance between us," Puffin said.

On a hill high above the lake, Jean-Bob and Speed looked up into the blue-black sky. The moon was just peeking over the horizon.

"No sign of them yet," Speed remarked.

"I hope zat pudgy Puffin knows what he's doing," Jean-Bob said.

But Speed's eyes were focussed on a pair of dots that had risen above the distant treetops. "Incoming!" he called out.

Jean-Bob followed his gaze to the sight of Odette and Puffin, fast coming closer.

"Bring them in, Jean-Bob!" Speed said.

Jean-Bob plucked two fireflies out of the sky. Holding them like torches, he waved them toward a clear pathway to the lake.

Odette and Puffin changed course. They headed downward, toward Jean-Bob.

As they lit on the rock, all eyes were riveted on the moon. The rising disk now flecked the tree-tops with white light. Below them, the lake still lay in darkness.

Derek stepped out of the forest, onto the shore of the lake. Bow in hand, he looked around in wonder, taking in the water, the ravaged castle . . .

Hidden on the hill above him, Odette, Puffin, and Jean-Bob watched Derek in silence. Their plan had worked!

"It's almost time, Odette," Puffin said softly. "Look!"

Moonlight washed over the trees, slowly making its way to the lake.

"I — I can't do it!" Odette cried.

"You have to!" Puffin retorted.

"He'll kill me, Puffin, he'll kill me!"

"If you don't do it now, Odette, you've lost your chance for life!" Puffin replied. "Now, be brave!"

Gently, supportively, Puffin placed his wing on Odette's back.

The light was traveling faster now, spilling over the ridge of trees, crawling across the stone floor toward the water . . .

"Go!"

Puffin's voice was firm. Odette knew she had no choice. She spread her wings and lifted into the sky.

Derek turned. His eyes locked on the swooping white bird. He watched, frozen, as Odette landed on the lake.

"*Whaaaat?*" he murmured.

Yes, Odette thought. Derek's shock had delayed him. After chasing her so many miles, he hadn't expected her to fly right to him.

The opposite shore was now bathed in moonlight. The light crept closer . . . closer . . .

Derek raised his bow. He lifted it to his shoulder. Odette could see his piercing brown eye looking over the point of his arrow.

The light was only a few feet from the water now. Odette looked to the sky.

A thick clot of clouds nudged the moon.

Odette gasped.

Not now . . . not now!

Derek tensed his bowstring.

Then like a giant hand, the clouds blotted out the moon.

At the edge of the lake shore, the light disappeared.

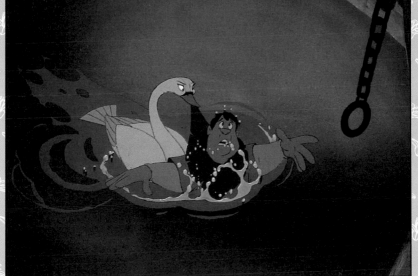

11

"*CAAAAAAW!*"
Puffin's cry echoed through the forest. He bombed from the sky, hitting Derek full-force.

The arrow flew wildly into the lake, over Odette's head.

Derek and Puffin rolled in the dirt, squawking and shouting. Puffin flapped his wings, smacking the Prince, trying to distract him.

But Derek seized him and tossed him aside. Springing to his feet, Derek loaded another arrow onto his bow.

Odette thought about flying away. But the clouds were passing. The moon was peeking through, shining dully on the lakeshore again. The light inched closer . . .

Derek held his breath. He pointed his arrow at Odette.

And closer . . .

Derek's eyes were determined and murderous. This time he would not miss.

59

And closer . . .

"Gotcha!" he said.

Odette closed her eyes.

SWWWWWISHHH!

She felt water and light rising around her. Shielding her. Swirling upward . . .

The forest was blotted out by the whirlpool of silver-blue. Derek disappeared from sight.

Where was the arrow? Did he shoot?

Odette felt nothing. She was floating now. Growing. Soon she couldn't feel any feathers at all.

Then the water and light vanished.

Her eyes blinked open. The first thing she noticed was Derek's face — eyes wide, jaw open with amazement.

Odette smiled. She was standing on solid ground. She was human.

"Hello, Derek," she said.

The bow and arrow dropped from Derek's hand. He was transforming, too. From an angry, vengeful hunter to a young man insane with joy.

They ran into each other's arms. Derek's embrace took away the pain, the fright, the unbearable gloom of the last day.

"Oh, Odette, I *knew* it — you're alive!" Derek said, his voice thick with emotion. "No one believed me, but I knew!"

"Sshhh!" Odette warned him. "You can't stay."

"I didn't mean to shoot you. I thought you were

the Great Animal — " Derek pulled back and looked her in the eye. "Can't stay? No! I'll never let you out of my sight!"

"Listen to me, Derek — " Odette began.

From the direction of the castle, Rothbart's voice thundered: "*Odette!*"

"Oh, no!" Odette cried in horror.

"Who is it?" Derek asked. "What's going on?"

"It's him!"

"Who?"

"He has me under a spell!"

"Who does?"

"*Odette!*" Rothbart called again.

Derek drew his sword. "Let him come! I'll —"

"No!" Odette replied. "He has great power! You must go!"

"Then you're coming with me!"

"I can't. When the moon sets, I'll turn back into a swan."

"*Odette!*" The voice was getting closer now.

"Go!" Odette pushed Derek toward the woods.

"There must be some way to break the spell."

"There is," Odette replied. "You must make a vow of everlasting love."

"I make it! I make it," Derek said.

Odette was growing more and more frightened for him. "You must prove it to the world."

"How?" Derek asked.

"I don't know," said Odette as she frantically shoved him to safety.

61

Derek turned to leave, then whirled suddenly around. His face was radiant. "The ball!" he blurted. "Tomorrow night, come to the castle. I will choose you. I will make a vow of everlasting love!"

Tears welled up in Odette's eyes. Derek had risked his life for her. He had searched through the forest for the beast that killed her father, not knowing who or what it was.

Now he was saying the words she had longed to hear. And for the first time, she felt hope.

"*ODETTE!*" Rothbart bellowed.

"I'm coming!" Odette shouted back. Then she turned to Derek and whispered, "Go!"

"Tomorrow night!" Derek reminded her. But he didn't go. Instead he drew himself closer.

Their lips met, and Odette wanted to be a swan again — a giant swan, so she could fly away with Derek on her back.

"Yes," Odette replied in the Prince's ear. "To-morrow night. Now, go!"

Grabbing one last precious instant, Derek kissed her again. Then he sped away and was swallowed up by the darkness of the forest.

Rothbart crashed through the woods to her left. He glared at her, breathing heavily. His sweaty hair was streaked across his forehead and his skin was red with exertion.

He did not look happy.

"Didn't you hear me calling?" he asked.

"I — I — " Odette stammered.

"I thought I heard voices."

Puffin, Jean-Bob, and Speed huddled together in the underbrush, watching the scene. Using his deepest frog-voice, Jean-Bob croaked, *"O-dette. O-dette."*

Odette swallowed hard. "Voices?"

"Yes, voices." Rothbart looked over his shoulder.

"Oh, um . . . I — "

Rothbart stepped toward the woods, peering intently. Odette panicked. How far could he see? Was his vision magical, too?

She had to distract him. "I — I've decided to become your queen!"

Rothbart turned to face her. His eyes were narrow and wary.

Behind a bush, Jean-Bob fainted at the news.

Rothbart's voice was hushed and awestruck. "You mean . . . oh, Odette!" He took her hand and kneeled. "I'll be a good king. You'll see. I'll wear nice clothes and I'll get the beard trimmed and — oh, Odette, you've made me so happy!"

With that, he stood and walked back toward the castle.

Odette looked toward her animal friends. Speed and Puffin peeked out from behind the bush, smiling. *They* knew why she'd lied to Rothbart.

"Oh, by the way . . ." Rothbart said.

Odette quickly turned to face him. He was

standing almost exactly where Derek had stood during Odette's transformation.

"You wouldn't happen to know who this belongs to, would you?" From the folds of his cape, Rothbart took out a bow.

Derek's bow.

Jean-Bob, who had just come to, fainted again.

Odette felt herself growing numb.

" 'Come to the ball! I will make a vow of everlasting love!' " Rothbart threw his head back and cackled. With a mighty thrust, he threw the bow into the lake. "Thought you could fool Rothbart, did you?"

"I will never be yours, you creature!" Odette shot back. "I will marry Prince Derek, and you cannot stop me!"

Rothbart's face turned red. His lips pulled back over his teeth like an angry animal. He grabbed her arms with all his strength.

But Odette had no fear. She locked eyes with him. At moonrise tomorrow she would be human again, and Rothbart would be powerless against her. Tomorrow she'd be free.

Rothbart took a deep breath and let go of Odette. His snarl vanished and he chuckled. "I hate to tell you this, Odette, but you won't be able to attend the big ball tomorrow night."

"If you want to stop me," Odette replied, "you'll have to kill me."

"I don't think so. You see, you've forgotten one very important thing."

Rothbart's smile chilled Odette to the bone.

"Tomorrow," he said, "there is no moon."

With that, Rothbart strolled back to his castle, shrieking with triumph.

12

"Oohhh-ha-ha-ha-hee-hee-hee-hee!" The Hag screamed with laughter as Rothbart told her what had just happened.

"No matter what they do," he declared, "I'm always one step ahead!"

The two of them howled.

But Rothbart suddenly grew serious. "On the other hand, Prince Derek's vow could ruin everything."

The Hag nodded.

"I'm going to have to deal with him." Rothbart began pacing. "But how?"

The Hag shrugged.

"The vow!" Rothbart said. "I'll get Derek to offer his vow to the wrong princess!"

The Hag looked confused.

"Don't you see?" Rothbart asked. "I'll make *you* look like Odette!"

Slowly the idea sank in. The Hag gave Rothbart a huge, gap-toothed smile.

"That's going to take a lot of work," Rothba[r] barged on, "but it'll be worth it, because whe[r] Derek makes his vow to the wrong girl, Odette will die! Then I'll finish him off myself." He laughed again. "Oh, I love it! I mean, this is really classy! This is *me*!"

At sunup the next day, Queen Uberta's castle sprang to life. Servants swarmed in and out, cleaning, dusting, washing, trimming. Candles were replaced, carpets were beaten, mirrors were scrubbed. Every crystal on every chandelier had to sparkle like a diamond.

The ball of all balls was only hours away.

In the ballroom, Lord Rogers and his musicians prepared for a rehearsal, while Uberta busily inspected the floral arrangements.

Derek burst through the door. "Mother, have you — ?"

"Oh, Derek, there you are," Uberta said.

"What are these?" Derek asked, gesturing to a bouquet.

Uberta looked at him oddly. "Roses."

"They're red."

"Of *course* they're red!"

"But, Mom, I don't want red roses. I want *white*, like a swan."

"White roses? Whatever for?"

"Because white is pure. It's *delicate*, like a — a swan."

'A swan," Uberta repeated dryly.

"Yeah. Have you seen Bromley?"

"No."

Derek called out to the servants, "Anyone seen Bromley?"

Chauncey, a butler, passed by with a tray of small, brownish meat chunks.

"What's this?" Derek asked.

"The appetizer," Chauncey replied.

Derek sneered. "No, no, no! Would you feed this to a swan?"

Chauncey gaped. "Uhhh . . ."

"Take it back!" Derek commanded. "Something *light*, something *fresh!*"

OOM-pah-pah, OOM-pah-pah . . . As Lord Rogers lowered his baton, the orchestra began blatting a loud waltz.

"No, no, no!" Derek shouted. "Hold it!"

Lord Rogers turned from the conductor's podium as the players stopped. Queen Uberta looked at her son as if he'd lost his mind.

"What's wrong?" Rogers asked.

"Everything," Derek replied. "It's *all* wrong. Tonight the music must be played *rubato*. Soft and graceful. Like a swan. Have you ever seen a swan, Rogers?"

"Of course I've seen a swan."

"If you could play a swan, what would it sound like?"

Rogers smiled. "Honking."

"*Soft* and *graceful*, Rogers," Derek said sternly. Then he turned to survey the room. "Where is Bromley?"

"No one has seen him, Derek," Uberta replied.

"You're kidding. Who's going to be my best man?"

"B- b- best — " Uberta was shocked speechless — well, almost. "You mean . . . you — "

Derek gave his mother a wink.

The orchestra swung into a lilting ballad.

"There you go, Rogers!" Derek called out. "That's the stuff!"

He hopped on the podium, took the baton from Rogers, and began conducting himself. "That's it! That's it!"

Then, handing the baton back to Rogers, he leaped off the platform and danced. Alone. Grinning wildly. Holding his arms out as if he had a partner.

Around the room, everyone stopped and gaped.

"Come on, Mother!" Derek swept Queen Uberta into his arms.

Uberta laughed as they danced across the room. "Don't be so secretive, Derek," she urged. "Tell me who it is!"

Laughing, Derek took Uberta's roses and flung them high in the air. His secret would keep until the night.

Long-stemmed roses splashed into the warm, foul water around Odette. High in the dank water dungeon tower, Rothbart hung out of an opening that led into his castle. As he dropped the roses, one by one, his sigh echoed off the stone walls.

"It hurts me to lock you up, Odette," he said. "Hurts me deep. But then, a king has to do what a king has to do."

Odette hated being confined in this dark, horrible place. Angrily she picked up a rose with her beak and snapped it in two.

"Aw, now you're mad at me again!" Rothbart mocked. "Doggone it, can't do *nothing* right. Head full of pudding, that's me."

Odette swam sullenly around, ignoring him.

"Well, I can't leave you like this," Rothbart went on. "If you're not happy, I'm not happy." He thought a minute, then snapped his fingers. "I know! If you can't attend the ball, I'll bring the ball to you! Let's see . . . the first thing you'll need is a young man. The Prince is busy, of course, but I think I can arrange a substitute."

Odette looked up. She could hear grunts and scuffling from a door next to Rothbart. Into the opening stepped Bromley!

His eyes bugged out as he gazed downward. "No, please! I beg you!"

"Poor fellow got lost in the woods," Rothbart said.

The Hag planted her foot on Bromley's backside and pushed.

"Nooo!" Bromley teetered at the edge, windmilling his arms.

Then, shrieking, he fell.

With a hugh splash, he plunged into the water. Odette swam to him as fast as she could.

His head bobbed up and he flailed crazily. "Hellllp! I can't swim!"

Odette bit his shirt and pulled him to the dungeon wall. There he grabbed onto the jagged edge of one of the stones.

"Don't leave me here!" Bromley cried.

"I'd love to stay," Rothbart replied, "but if I don't leave now, I'll be late for the ball, and that's tacky."

He gave Odette a sharp, angry glare. "Don't give me that look, Missy. Had to be sneaky and drag your weakling Prince into it, didn't you? Well, fine with me!"

Rothbart withdrew into the castle. His cackling filtered into the water dungeon. It mixed with Bromley's sobs and made Odette's blood run cold.

13

The Chamberlain burst into the Royal Dressing Room. "Excuse me, Your Highness. It's getting rather crowded outside."

Queen Uberta rose from her seat. Her elaborate silver hairdo added two feet to her height. "Very well. You may begin the introductions. And Chamberlain, no mistakes this time. Everything must be perfect."

"Oh, yes, Ma'am. Perfect."

He dashed out the door, tightly holding his stack of invitations.

Uberta turned to Derek, who was buttoning his shirtsleeves. "Promise me, Derek, that you'll tell me who it is the moment she arrives."

"Don't worry, Mother, you'll know," Derek replied. "Believe me, you'll know."

Puffin paced outside the water dungeon, deep in thought. "It's coming . . ." he muttered.

Jean-Bob and Speed watched him patiently. "What is?" Jean-Bob asked.

"An idea," Puffin answered. "A substantial idea. A large, colossal idea."

"Sounds big," Speed said.

Puffin stopped walking, his eyes growing large. *"I've got it!* Water leaks into the dungeon, right? Well, if there's a leak, there must be a hole. And if there's a hole — "

"If zere's a hole," Jean-Bob said, "Odette would've come out already."

"Not if it was a very tiny hole," Puffin countered. "We'll find the hole, make it bigger, and *ppphhew* her loose!"

"I think you're forgetting something." Jean-Bob opened his mouth and snapped it shut, imitating an alligator.

"His Majesty's got a point," Speed said.

"Not to worry, Puffin's in charge!" Puffin announced. "Okay, first we need a scout."

"Are you crazy?" Jean-Bob said. "Who are you going to find to jump into zis moat?"

Puffin looked at Jean-Bob. "He's got to be a good swimmer."

"I should say so!" Jean-Bob declared.

"He's got to be small, too," Speed suggested.

"Teeny-weeny," Jean-Bob agreed. "Not to be seen!"

"And it wouldn't hurt if he were green," Puffin continued, "for camouflage purposes."

"Precisely! Small, good swimmer, green — "
Jean-Bob stopped in mid-sentence. "Good grief!
Are you talking about *me*?"

"And you thought getting the map was fun."
Puffin began pacing again. "Now, the first thing
we'll do is create a diversion."

"No! Stop it!" Jean-Bob protested. "Absolutely
not!"

"That's where you come into play, Jean-Bob —"
Puffin went on.

"I can't hear you!" Jean-Bob cried.

Puffin calmly put his wing around Jean-Bob and
pulled the frog close. "Now, here's what I want
you to do . . ."

WHOMP! The Chamberlain shut the heavy oak
door to the castle ballroom. Every princess had
arrived. He had counted carefully.

With a smile, the Chamberlain descended the
grand staircase. The princesses stood about, each
lovelier than the one next to her. Bedecked with
jewels, they outshone the brilliant chandeliers.

One by one, they danced with Derek to the
strains of the royal orchestra.

It was perfect. Just as the Queen had re-
quested. The Chamberlain held his chin high.

Finally, after the last dance, Queen Uberta approached her son. "Well, Derek?" she asked ex-
pectantly.

Boom! Boom! Boom!

The Chamberlain jumped. Who could be knocking at the ballroom door now?

Queen Uberta scowled at him. "Chamberlain? All who were invited are present, are they not?"

The Chamberlain's hands shook as he looked through the invitations. "I — I — Yes! I mean, Katherine of Tearean, Anne of Wilshire, Constance of — yes, I'm sure that — "

Boom! Boom! Boom!

The Queen's face was reddening with rage. "I certainly hope that you have not locked someone out."

"Me, too," the Chamberlain said with a gulp. He ran up the steps and pulled the door open.

The entire ballroom fell silent. Derek stared in awe.

A princess walked into the light. Her beauty made all the others look plain. Her gown shimmered, throwing a radiant halo around her.

She made it, Derek said to himself with rising ecstasy. *Odette made it. And this time, I won't let her leave.*

Smiling, thrilled that the disguise was working, the Hag slowly walked down the stairs.

14

"**I**t can't be," Queen Uberta said under her breath.

Derek moved toward the stairs. Around him, the guests murmured in disbelief.

Uberta leaned toward the podium. "Rogers! Who is it? Do you know her?"

"I . . . don't know," Rogers replied.

"Come now, Rogers," Uberta said. "I know he confides in you. Who is it?"

"I promise, I do not know her. Although she does look a great deal like — "

"But it couldn't be!" Queen Uberta squinted at the young lady, whose face so resembled the poor, dead daughter of King William. "Could it?"

Derek approached his beloved. He reached out and touched her soft cheek. "I was so worried," he said, beaming. "I almost thought — "

"Nothing could keep me away," the Hag replied.

Derek turned to Lord Rogers and snapped his fingers twice. Immediately Rogers cued his orchestra.

As Derek's song filled the ballroom, he began to dance with the girl of his dreams.

A few yards from the moat, Puffin rubbed Jean-Bob's shoulders. "Okay. Speed will draw the gators away. Then you'll get a running start and *psshhew* for that hole."

"*If* I can find it," Jean-Bob said nervously, "And if ze alligators don't chew me before I get zere!"

"Don't worry," Puffin assured him," Speed will rush to help."

"Suddenly, I'm full of comfort."

Puffin raised his wing high. Across the moat, Speed waited for his signal.

"On your mark!" Puffin bellowed.

Jean-Bob shook out his legs and crouched into a sprinter's position.

Speed began shouting at the alligators, "Hey, you old leatherheads, come and get me! Come on, bug eyes! This way, chicken lips!"

The alligators turned. They floated angrily toward Speed.

"Perfect!" Puffin said. "Okay, ready . . . set . . . go!"

Jean-Bob bounded toward the moat.

"Faster!" Puffin urged. "Faster!"

*   *   *

Higher and higher Jean-Bob leaped. "Sure," he muttered to himself. "Go on, Jean-Bob, race to your death!"

The alligators were floating in Speed's direction. Their backs were to Jean-Bob.

But not for long.

One of them looked backward for a moment. His eyes met Jean-Bob's. Instantly he turned.

Jean-Bob tried to pull up short. But he was going too fast.

With a terrified scream, he bounced into the water.

When he rose to the surface, he was looking into the eyes of two hungry alligators.

"Waaaaah!" He began swimming for his life.

Zzzzzooom! Speed whizzed by him. "Get moving, slowpoke!" he called to Jean-Bob.

"Slowpoke?" Jean-Bob said.

The alligators tore past him, intent on catching Speed.

So *that* was how the turtle got his nickname!

Jean-Bob dove underwater. He swam to the wall of the water dungeon. He examined it, block by block. Where was the opening?

"Any luck?" came Speed's voice.

Jean-Bob looked around. Before he could answer, a wall of alligators swam into view. Speed darted out of the way.

This time, the alligators didn't go after him.

They headed straight for Jean-Bob.

Jean-Bob had no time to think. If he didn't do something drastic, he was dinner for sure.

The hole.

He could barely see it. But there it was, impossibly tiny, leaking between two loose stones at the base of the tower.

Thrusting his legs, he shot into the tiny opening.

Thook. He made it halfway.

"Arrrrgh . . ." Jean-Bob twisted, but his body only jammed tighter and tighter.

He was stuck!

15

S *queeak! Squeeak!*

With all his strength, Jean-Bob inched his body further and further inward.

His legs disappeared into the hole. An alligator lunged after him, chomping down fiercely.

It crashed into the tower wall.

BOOOM! The impact shook the tower. Stones broke loose. Jean-Bob blasted like a rocket through the wall.

He shot through the water inside the tower, and straight up above the surface.

Hanging over the water was a rusted iron ring. Jean-Bob grabbed it and hung on.

"Jean-Bob!" cried Odette, floating below him.

Jean-Bob smiled weakly. "To the rescue, mademoiselle!"

Outside the tower, Puffin stood on a tree branch and watched. Speed was still leading the alligators around the tower.

Suddenly the turtle rose into the air and spur

"There's the signal," Puffin said to himself. "Al right, Puffin, time to brush up on diving technique."

He launched himself downward.

SPLASHHH!

When Puffin rose to the surface, the alligators were staring at him.

"How about a little white meat?" Puffin taunted. "Good for the heart!"

As the alligators chased Puffin, Speed plunged downward. He found Jean-Bob's hole and began digging.

Yes! The alligators had loosened the stones. Speed began clearing them away with his claws. Quickly the hole widened.

From his hanging ring, Jean-Bob leaped into the water. He dove to the hole and spotted Speed pushing away stones.

Jean-Bob raced to the surface. "We broke through!" he called to Odette.

"Oh, Jean-Bob, thank you!" Odette replied. "When all this is over, remind me to give you a kiss."

Jean-Bob beamed. "Ha *haaa!*" he crowed, punching a fist into the air.

Odette swam to Bromley. She knew she would face one big problem: humans could not understand animal speech.

She grabbed his shirt with her bill and pulled.

"What? What is it?" Bromley said, his eyes wide with fright. "Stay away! What are you doing? *NO!* Get away!"

Odette let go. She stared at him. He was Derek's best friend, but he was frozen with fear.

And she had no time to waste.

She plunged into the water and swam hard.

Speed saw her and held up a hand. "I'll tell you when," he said.

He stuck his head out of the hole just as Puffin's webbed feet swam by — followed by madly paddling alligator legs.

Speed looked back to Odette. "Let's go!"

He squeezed out. Odette followed close behind.

The first thing she saw as she emerged was a pair of eyes, yellow and hungry.

And a gaping mouth full of pointed teeth!

SNAP!

Odette ducked back into the hole as the alligator bit down.

That was close.

She shot out of the hole. With a powerful leg thrust, she swam for the surface.

SNAP!

Now another alligator was after her.

She pulled away, losing a few feathers.

Speed lurched into action, knocking one alligator away.

Odette splashed through the surface. Behind

her rose another alligator, jaws wide, ready to close around her.

Beside him rose Puffin. Hunching his body, he struck at the alligator with his webbed feet.

The alligator fell back into the moat.

And Odette, throwing off water in a jet stream, took to the air!

16

Derek and his Princess swirled around the ballroom. The other guests stared enviously. Queen Uberta was sobbing with joy.

Derek looked deeply into the eyes of Odette. Their blue color was as deep as he remembered. Her hair shone like firelight, just as before. She was perfect.

Almost.

A moment before, he had been dizzy with happiness. But that had faded.

Something wasn't right.

Derek managed a shy smile. "Odette, you seem . . . I don't know, *different*," he said.

The Hag smiled. From inside her gown, she pulled out her locket — the locket Prince Derek had given Odette as a child. "Don't worry," she reassured him. "After tonight, everything will be perfect."

Derek fingered the old locket. She had saved it

her whole life. Truly she loved him. How could he have doubted her?

As the couple danced near the orchestra, Derek tapped Lord Rogers on the shoulder. "Rogers," he said, "I have to make an announcement."

With an obedient nod, Rogers stopped the music.

The guests applauded politely as Derek bowed to his partner. He took her hand and squeezed it gently. Then he led her up the red-carpeted ballroom stairs.

All guests watched, whispering in anticipation. Queen Uberta wiped tears from her eyes. A few of the other Princesses could not cover up the envy in their eyes.

At the top of the stairs, Derek turned. He raised his arms, quieting the crowd's murmur.

"Kings and Queens, Ladies and Gentlemen!" he called out. "And, of course, Mother."

Uberta smiled and daubed her cheek with a handkerchief.

"I have an announcement to make," Derek went on. "Today I have found my bride."

Outside the ballroom window, under the moonless sky, Odette hovered, panting for breath.

It couldn't be true. Derek was holding her hand. Announcing his engagement.

"No," she whispered.

Her wings, tired from the flight, began to batter the window. "No, Derek!" she cried. "It's a trick!"

No one could hear her. "And now," Derek was saying, "before the whole world, I make a vow to break all vows."

Odette flew to a closer window and banged again. "No! Derek! Over here! *Derek!*"

From window to window Odette flew, trying to attract attention.

But all eyes were on Derek and his love.

". . . A vow," Derek continued, "that is stronger than all the powers in the earth."

"DEREK, PLEASE!" Odette was right above him now. He had to hear. *"DON'T DO IT! IT'S A TRICK! DEREK!"*

"I make a vow of everlasting love . . ." Derek turned to the imposter with a rapturous smile. "To Odette!"

The applause was instant. The castle seemed to explode from within.

And so did Odette's heart. She hovered, staring in shock.

He had declared his love to someone else.

Odette would remain forever a swan, forever loveless.

She raised her head skyward. An anguished cry welled up from the depths of her imprisoned body.

And then she went limp, falling to the earth.

17

WHAM! Above Derek, a window smashed open.

WHAM! WHAM! WHAM!

Around the ballroom, one by one, the other windows swung inward.

An icy wind whipped through the room. Screams rang out.

Bewildered, Derek looked around.

BOOOMMM!

The ballroom door flew open. Against the inky darkness, his cape billowing in the wind, stood Rothbart.

"Hello, Little Prince."

Derek held his ground. He stood face-to-face with Rothbart. "Who are you?" he asked defiantly.

Rothbart cackled. "Went and pledged your love to another, eh?"

"What are you talking about? This is Odette!"

"No," Rothbart replied. "Odette is mine."

Now Derek knew who this stranger was. Only one person could make that claim. Only the Enchanter who killed King William and cast the spell on his princess.

"You," Derek said. "You're powerless here. I made a vow — a vow of everlasting love!"

"You made a vow all right," Rothbart mocked. "A vow of everlasting *death!*"

Rothbart raised his right arm and sent forth a blast of harsh light. It hit Derek's beautiful partner, spreading over her entire body.

The guests gasped in horror.

"No!" Derek shouted.

The young Princess fell to the ground, head down. Derek ran to her. He cradled her in his arms, lifting her head. Turning her to see if her face showed signs of life.

Her blond hair fell over his arms.

And Derek was staring into the thick, warty face of a grinning, foul-breathed Hag!

Derek jumped to his feet. Odette! Where was Odette? Who was —

"You should have left her to me!" Rothbart said. "Now, Odette will die!"

"*EEEE-AH-HA-HA!*" the Hag shrieked, pointing to a window.

Derek turned to look. In the receding glow of the ballroom light, a dim white form flew slowly away from the castle.

A swan.

"Odette," Derek said, his voice choked and weak.

His feet propelled him out the castle door. He turned in the direction he'd seen the swan and shouted:

"ODETTE!"

But the white form was gone.

18

Derek ran to the stable and mounted his horse.

"If you hurry, Little Prince," Rothbart called from the castle door, "I'll let you see her one last time!"

But Derek was not listening. *"Odette!"* he cried once more, urging his horse into a gallop.

The sharp wind tore against him as he rode across the castle lawn. The horse sped blindly into the forest, its feet barely touching the ground.

The trees loomed around Derek, black and dense. Through eyes slitted against the blinding gale, he maneuvered his horse around them. All the while he shouted the name of his beloved.

Not once did she answer. Not once did the swan appear overhead.

Deep in the woods, the trees seemed to crowd in. The horse faltered. She began to buck and shy, whinnying in fear.

Derek drew his sword and dismounted. Alone,

on foot, he bushwhacked through the under-growth.

"*She's fading fast!*"

Now Rothbart's voice was floating in the air like an evil spirit.

"No!" Derek shouted, slashing right and left.

Inside the water dungeon, Bromley clung to the small ledge, whimpering. He had heard the voice, too. Rothbart was getting closer.

The last place he wanted to be was in this stinking tower. Slowly he released his fingers from the rock and dove into the water.

Outside, Jean-Bob, Speed, and Puffin stood near the lake, looking upward. "Something's gone wrong," Puffin said.

"Zere she is!" Jean-Bob shouted.

Barely clearing the treetops, Odette flew to-ward them. Her wings flapped slowly and her body hung limp.

"I don't think she's going to make it," Speed remarked.

"*This way, Odette!*" Puffin shouted. "Just a lit-tle further!"

Jean-Bob and Speed joined the shouting. Odette perked up her head a bit. She tried to slow herself down, level out. But she was plunging heavily.

She glided over their heads and crashed into the stone floor by the lake.

The animals gathered around her motionless body.

"Is she still alive?" Speed asked.

"I don't know," Puffin replied.

Jean-Bob leaned over her. "Please, Odette. Don't die."

Her dull white form began to change. It started with a flicker of light that seemed to come from within. Then the light radiated outward, growing into a bright wash of red and white and orange and blue.

Jean-Bob, Speed, and Puffin backed off and watched.

When the light receded, the swan was gone. Now Odette the Princess was lying on the stone.

At the edge of the woods, Derek emerged from the thick darkness. He stopped for a moment, panting, hardly able to stand.

The animals looked at him sadly. None of them was able to say a word.

Derek glanced around. His eyes locked on Odette. With new strength, he sprinted to her side and dropped to his knees.

"Odette," he said, lifting her head into his chest. "What have I done to you? Forgive me, Odette. Forgive me."

Hearing his voice, Odette stirred. She struggled to open her eyes.

"*Derek* . . ." Her voice was almost lost to the wind.

Derek looked into her face with hope, trying to catch her gaze.

"I feel so weak . . ." Odette murmured. "I think . . ."

"No, you'll *live*, Odette!" Derek stroked her hair tenderly, supporting her with his strong arms. "It's *you* I love. It's you! The vow I made was for you."

Derek set Odette down gently. He stood up and raised his despairing eyes to the heavens. To wherever Rothbart might be. *"I made the vow for her! Do you hear? THE VOW I MADE WAS FOR HER!"*

From behind him came a soft, grating voice. "No need to shout."

Derek snapped around to face Rothbart. "Don't let her die!"

Rothbart smiled. "Is that a threat?"

Derek stepped forward and grabbed the Enchanter by his cloak. "Don't you dare let her die," he hissed.

"Ooooh, it *is* a threat," Rothbart replied.

"You're the only one with the power. *Now, do it!*"

Rothbart laughed. "Only if you defeat me."

A wave of his arm sent a blaze of light into the night air. It wrapped around Rothbart, pulsing and brightening.

A blinding flash made Derek reel backward.

When he looked up, Rothbart was a towering, snarling beast.

"The Great Animal," Derek said.

The creature bellowed so loud, the trees seemed to bend.

Cowering behind a rock, Jean-Bob said to Speed and Puffin, "I'm betting on the animal."

"I won't let her die!" Derek shouted. He picked up his sword and ran it into the beast.

"*YEEEAAAAAAGHHH!*" thundered the Great Animal.

As if plucking a small weed, the Great Animal lifted Derek off the ground, then tossed him down the stone stairs that led to the lake.

Derek's sword flew out of his hand. He landed in shallow water. Before he could stand, the Great Animal attacked again.

Derek struggled to his feet. He clamped his hands around the creature's neck and tried to squeeze.

RRRAAAGHH! With its massive beak, the Great Animal tore into Derek's shoulder.

"Odette!" Derek yelled, falling to the ground.

The Great Animal thrust itself into the air, then landed on Derek, grabbing him in its talons.

Behind the rock, Puffin suddenly shouted to his cohorts: "The bow! Swim to the bottom of the lake and get the bow!"

Puffin grabbed Speed and hurled him into the lake. Jean-Bob jumped in after him.

Above them soared the Great Animal, with

Derek in its clutches. Crying out in triumph, it flung Derek into a sturdy pine tree.

With a sickening thump, Derek smacked against it and tumbled to the forest floor.

He tried to stand. Grimacing in pain, he fell, unconscious.

At the bottom of the lake, Jean-Bob saw the bow stuck in a tangle of weeds. He pulled frantically, but it wouldn't move.

In an instant, Speed was by his side. Together they yanked once . . . twice . . .

The bow jerked upward, out of the muck. Speed took it and swam to the water's surface. Jean-Bob, still holding the bow, was dragged along with him.

As their faces broke through the surface, they looked for Derek.

He lay limp on the ground.

The Great Animal circled above him, ready to descend for the kill.

19

"**T**hrow it!" Puffin shouted. "Throw it!"

Speed reared back and threw. Still clutching the bow, Jean-Bob went flying with it.

"Whoooooa!" Jean-Bob cried.

With a jolt, bow and frog landed on the stone floor near Derek.

Jean-Bob jumped on the Prince's head. "Wake up!" he said, lifting Derek's eyelids. "Hello?"

The shadow of the Great Animal grew larger around them.

"Good-bye," Jean-Bob said with a gulp. He leaped out of the way.

But Derek was stirring.

His eyes sprang open. The claws of the Great Animal were dropping toward him fast. Quickly he grabbed the bow. He reached over his back for an arrow.

And he realized he wasn't carrying any arrows.

"Oh, please . . . oh, please . . . oh, please . . ." a small voice piped up near the water dungeon.

"*Brom?*" Derek said.

Soaking wet, Bromley stood just outside the tower. He aimed at Derek's chest with his bow and arrow.

"*NOW!*" Bromley shouted.

Bromley released. The arrow sliced the air.

Derek spun around. With a snap of his wrist, he snatched the arrow out of the air. Loading it onto his bow, he pointed it upward.

The Great Animal stopped in midflight. Its evil yellow eyes whitened with fear.

Derek let fly.

Zzzzing! The arrow shot upward and planted itself in the creature's chest.

GRAAAAAAAWWWWWWW!

The cry swept over the lake with the force of a tornado. The beast seemed to hover, stuck in the air like an awful, misshapen balloon.

Then, slowly, it dropped into the lake.

For a moment the area fell silent. Not a rustling leaf was heard.

Then the Great Animal floated to the surface. Dead.

The stillness was broke by Jean-Bob, Puffin, and Speed. "*Yaaaa-hooooo!*" they shouted.

Bromley stood on the opposite shore, his mouth hanging open.

But Derek took no joy in his kill. He leaned over the lifeless body of his princess. The only true love of his life. The love he had given up.

The love that had blinded him to the evil trick of Rothbart.

Quietly weeping, he gathered her body in his arms. "Forgive me, Odette. I only wanted to break the spell. To prove my love." He choked back a sob. "I'll always love you."

The words seemed to float from his lips and bathe the dead princess. Color flowed into the ghostly white skin of her face. She felt lighter in Derek's arms.

And then, she moved.

Derek pushed her matted hair from her forehead. Could it be?

Slowly Princess Odette opened her eyes. "Oh, Derek!" she said, her voice faint.

"Odette!" Derek shouted.

Her arms closed around him. And he held her with all the strength and joy in his overflowing heart.

The animals turned to one another, trying not to cry.

"Well," Puffin said. "There you have it. Everlasting love."

20

B onnng! Bonnng!
The bells of the royal cathedral hadn't rung so loud in years.

Every house in the kingdom was empty. Not one townsperson would miss the wedding of Prince Derek to Princess Odette. They filled the cathedral, spilling into the streets.

Never before had a noise been heard like the roar that greeted the young husband and wife as they burst through the church door. The hats thrown joyously into the air created a momentary eclipse of the sun.

Lord Rogers and Bromley stood outside the church, watching the pandemonium.

"Well, Rogers, old man," Bromley remarked, "I suppose you owe me an apology. After all, if it weren't for me, the Great Animal would still be alive."

Behind Rogers's head, the shadow of a winged

beast appeared on the wall. Bromley's eyes widened as it loomed larger and larger.

"Dear me," Rogers gasped, staring at something over Bromley's shoulder. "No."

"Wh- what is it?" Bromley stammered.

"The Great Animal! It's alive!"

With a terrified cry, Bromley fainted to the floor.

Queen Uberta passed by Rogers, her elaborate swan wig balanced regally atop her head.

Rogers chuckled to himself. How fortunate the wig's shadow looked so gruesome.

"Uberta," he said with a grin.

"Rogers," Uberta replied warmly.

A few hours later, the reception at the new palace began. Derek and Odette marveled at how fast the Queen's subjects had renovated Rothbart's castle. Now it stood proudly over the water, scrubbed and inviting.

It now belonged to the Prince and Princess.

Above them swooped the new Royal Air Force — General Puffin and his army of swans!

As the party went on noisily inside, Odette stood near the lake with Jean-Bob and Speed. Jean-Bob looked up at the Princess, leaning toward her with his cheek. He wore a small, velvet cape.

"Don't be too disappointed, Jean-Bob, if nothing happens," Odette warned.

But Jean-Bob ignored her. "Finally, after all zese years," he said, "I shall return to my throne!"

"Don't forget to write," Speed said.

Jean-Bob glowered at him. "You still don't believe me, do you?"

"The only thing you're going to turn is *red*," Speed replied.

Jean-Bob looked defiantly at Odette. "I'm ready."

Odette leaned over and planted a gentle kiss on his cheek.

Jean-Bob spun around. His eyes rolled. He gasped. He doubled over, covering his face. Then he triumphantly raised himself to his full height.

He looked exactly the same.

"Ha!" he cried. "What do you have to say now, Speed?"

"Uh . . ." Speed began.

"Zat's what I *thought!*" Jean-Bob said. "And now, if you don't mind, I have some socializing to do!"

He threw his cape over his shoulder and strolled into the crowd. With a princely swagger he nodded to the guests. "Bonjour, madam . . . How are you today, sir? Hello, my little flower."

"Eeeek!" a young maiden screamed and dropped to the floor at the sight of a frog.

"Ha! I can still make zem faint!" Jean-Bob gloated.

As he disappeared into the party, Odette smiled at Speed. "Would you like a kiss, too?"

"Naw," Speed answered. "I'm happy as a turtle."

From behind them, Derek called out, "There you are!"

Odette turned to her Prince. He was smiling at her from the entrance to the castle. "There are still a hundred people waiting to see you inside," he said.

Odette sighed. "Well, I suppose there's only one thing we can do."

They looked at each other for a moment, then broke into wide smiles.

Laughing, they took each other's hands and ran — *away* from their new home.

In the clear glow of the moonlight, they glided across the vast lawn. They stopped only when they reached the new bridge that spanned the lake.

Derek twirled his bride in the air. As he set her down gently, she gazed into his eyes.

Below them, the lake lapped against the shore. In the distance, music and merry laughter rang out from the castle windows.

"Will you love me, Derek," Princess Odette asked, "until the day I die?"

"No," Derek replied. "Much longer than that, Odette. Much longer."

As they wrapped each other in a kiss, Odette knew he would live up to that promise.